For Karen,
dear friend
and fellow writer,
with my best wishes,
Love,
Valiska Gregory
1989

Mr. Poggle and Scamp
lived together
in a comfy house
in the middle
of the deep green woods.

In the bedroom
there were two beds.
At the table
there were two chairs.
And by the fireside
there were eight paws
with brown toasty toes.

Every day
was different,
and every day
was the same.

Every morning
the sun would open
his orange eye.
And every night
the sky would tuck
her dark blue blanket
over his nose.
But what happened
in between made
all the difference.

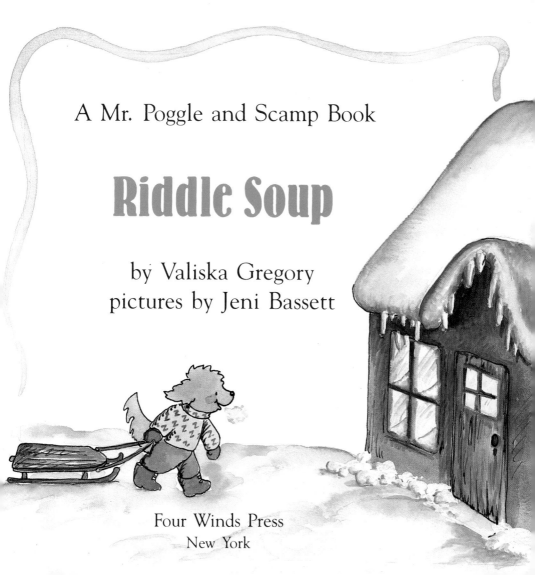

A Mr. Poggle and Scamp Book

# Riddle Soup

by Valiska Gregory
pictures by Jeni Bassett

Four Winds Press
New York

For my parents, with love—V.G.

For Nathan Smith—J.B.

LUCAS EVANS BOOKS

Text copyright © 1987 by Valiska Gregory
Illustrations copyright © 1987 by Jeni Bassett
Four Winds Press
Macmillan Publishing Company
866 Third Avenue, New York, NY 10022
Collier Macmillan Canada, Inc.
Printed and bound by South China Printing Company, Hong Kong
First American Edition
10 9 8 7 6 5 4 3 2 1
The text of this book is set in 14 pt. Goudy Old Style.
The illustrations are rendered in pen-and-ink and watercolor wash.

Library of Congress Cataloging-in-Publication Data
Gregory, Valiska.        Riddle soup. (A Mr. Poggle and Scamp book)
Summary: When Scamp complains they never have interesting suppers,
Mr. Poggle decides to make Riddle Soup. Recipe is included at the end of the story.
[1. Soups—Fiction. 2. Dogs—Fiction] I. Bassett, Jeni, ill.
II. Title. III. Series: Gregory, Valiska. Mr. Poggle and Scamp book.
PZ7.G8624Ri 1987        [E]        87-190
ISBN 0-02-738090-4        ISBN 0-02-738100-5 (pbk.)

"For supper today,"
said Mr. Poggle,
"we will have hot soup
and crusty fresh bread."
"Not again," said Scamp.
"I wish we could have
something interesting."

"Something interesting?"
asked Mr. Poggle.
He scratched the top
of his head.
"I know," he said.
"Today we will have
crusty fresh bread
and Riddle Soup."

"The bread part is
  the same," said Scamp.
"I know," said Mr. Poggle,
"but the soup part
  will keep you guessing."

He put the bread into
the oven and sizzled
butter in the pot.

"Now," he said,
"what is as long
    as an icicle,
    as round as a penny,
    and makes a good nose?"

"Can you give me a hint?"
asked Scamp.
"It is also orange,"
said Mr. Poggle.

"A carrot!" shouted Scamp.
"It is as long as an icicle
 and as round as a penny."

Scamp frowned. "But
it is *not* a good nose."

"Of course it is,"
said Mr. Poggle.
"A carrot is a wonderful
    nose—for a snowman."

He sliced the icicle carrots
into round carrot pennies
and put them into the pot.
"Now," said Mr. Poggle,
"what has lots of rings
but does not go ding-dong?"

Scamp frowned. "Can you
give me a hint?"
"It can also make you cry,"
said Mr. Poggle.

"An onion!" shouted Scamp.
They sliced the onion and
punched out the rings.

The onion made
their noses run and
their eyes water.

"I am laughing and crying
at the same time."
Scamp giggled.

He put the onions
into the pot.

"Now," said Mr. Poggle,
"what has leaves,
    is as straight as a tree,
    and sometimes looks
    like moon slivers?"
"Can you give me a hint?"
    asked Scamp.
"It is also crunchy,"
    said Mr. Poggle.

"Celery!" shouted Scamp.
Mr. Poggle sliced the celery
into green moon slivers
and put them into the pot.

They giggled and frowned
and riddled and sliced.

They put in potatoes
and peas and parsley.

They put in noodles
and pepper and salt.

"Now," said Scamp finally,
"I have one for you.
     What is as hungry as a bear
     and very good at riddles?"

"Can you give me a hint?"
asked Mr. Poggle.
"It's something that loves soup."
Scamp giggled.
Mr. Poggle grinned.
"I give up," he said.

"It's me!" shouted Scamp.
He blew on his soup to cool
it off. The steam danced
on top like question marks.

"Is Riddle Soup always this
interesting?" he asked.
Mr. Poggle took a sip.
"It is as interesting,"
he said, "as you make it."

# Riddle Soup

Make sure you have a grown-up help you. Sizzle 2 tablespoons of butter in a soup pot. Riddle* and slice the vegetables, put them into the pot, and stir for 3–4 minutes:

> ½ cup carrots, sliced into pennies
> ½ cup onions, sliced into rings
> ½ cup celery, sliced into moon slivers

Add and simmer for ½ hour with the lid on:

> 2 cups peeled and diced potatoes
> 1 cup peas (frozen or fresh)
> 2 tablespoons chopped parsley
> ½ cup noodles
> 6 cups chicken or beef broth
> a pinch of salt and pepper

*Hint: A good riddle tells what something is like if you look at it carefully. Is a pea like a green marble? Like a winter berry? Remember, Riddle Soup is only as interesting as you make it.